Praise for
KRISTINE KATHRYN RUSCH'S
DIVING UNIVERSE

"The Diving Universe, conceived by Hugo-Award winning author Kristine [Kathryn] Rusch is a refreshingly new and fleshed out realm of sci-fi action and adventure."
—*Astroguyz*

"Kristine Kathryn Rusch is best known for her Retrieval Artist series, so maybe you've missed her Diving Universe series. If so, it's high time to remedy that oversight."
—*Analog*

"This is classic sci-fi, a well-told tale of dangerous exploration. The first-person narration makes the reader an eye witness to the vast, silent realms of deep space, where even the smallest error will bring disaster. Compellingly human and technically absorbing, the suspense builds to fevered intensity, culminating in an explosive yet plausible conclusion."
—*RT Book Reviews* (Top Pick) on *Diving into the Wreck*

"Rusch delivers a page-turning space adventure while contemplating the ethics of scientists and governments working together on future tech."
—*Publishers Weekly* on *Diving into the Wreck*

The Diving Universe
(Reading Order)

THE APPLICATION *OF* HOPE

A DIVING UNIVERSE NOVELLA

KRISTINE KATHRYN RUSCH

*wmg*PUBLISHING

The Application of Hope

Published 2021 by WMG Publishing
www.wmgpublishing.com
First published in *Asimov's SF Magazine,* August 2013
Book and cover design copyright © 2021 by WMG Publishing
Cover design by Allyson Longueira/WMG Publishing
Cover art copyright © Philcold
ISBN-13: 978-1-56146-340-4
ISBN-10: 1-56146-340-X

THE APPLICATION OF HOPE

A DIVING UNIVERSE NOVELLA

1

"Requesting support. The *Ivoire*, just outside of Ukhanda's orbit. Need warships."

The calmness in the request caught Captain Tory Sabin's ear before the name of the ship registered. She had stopped on the bridge just briefly, on her way to a dinner she had sponsored for her support staff. She wasn't dressed like a captain. She had decided to stay out of her uniform and wear an actual dress for a change.

At least she had on practical shoes.

But she felt odd as she hurried across the nearly empty bridge, covered in perfume, her black hair curled on the top of her head, her grandmother's antique rivets-and-washers bracelet jingling on her left wrist. She grabbed the arm of the captain's chair, but didn't sit down.

Only three people stood on the bridge—the skeleton crew, all good folks, all gazing upwards as if the voice of Jonathon "Coop" Cooper, captain of the *Ivoire*, were speaking from the ceiling.

Then Lieutenant Perry Graham, a man whose reddish blond hair and complexion made him look continually embarrassed, leaned forward. He tapped the console in front of him, so that he could bring up the *Ivoire's* location.

It came up in a 2-D image, partly because of the distance, and partly because Graham—the consummate professional—knew that Sabin preferred her long-distance views flat rather than in three dimensions. The best members of any bridge crew learned how to accommodate their captain's quirks as well as her strengths.

She moved closer to the wall screen displaying the image. The ship, marked in shining gold (the default setting for the entire Fleet), showed up in small relief, traveling quickly. Like Coop had said, the *Ivoire* wasn't too far from the planet Ukhanda. Whatever was causing the crisis wasn't readily apparent from this distant view, but Sabin could tell just from Coop's voice that he had been under attack.

Coop was one of those men, one of those *captains*, who didn't ask for help if he could avoid it. Much as she teased him about this, she knew she fell in that category as well.

Sabin didn't have to tell Graham to zoom in. He did, more than once, until the *Ivoire* looked huge. Around it were at least a dozen other ships, so small and feathery that they almost seemed like errors in the image.

"What the hell?" said Second Lieutenant Megan Phan. She was tiny and thin, her angular face creased with a frown. She probably hadn't even realized that she had spoken out loud.

Sabin doubted the other two had realized it either. Phan's words probably echoed their thoughts. In all her years in the Fleet, Sabin had never seen ships like that.

On screen, they looked too small to do any damage. If they were firing on the *Ivoire*, it wasn't obvious. But their position suggested an attack, and a rather vicious one.

"Let Captain Cooper know we're on the way," Sabin said to Graham.

"Yes, sir," Graham said, and sent the word.

The *Geneva*'s current rotation put it in the front line of defense for the Fleet, but the Fleet was in a respite period, which was why Sabin only had a skeleton crew on board. The Fleet had rendezvoused near an unoccupied moon. Six hundred of the Fleet's ships were engaged in maintenance, meetings, and vacations, all on a rotating schedule.

She'd been in dozens of respite periods like this one, and she'd never needed more than a few officers on the bridge.

Until now.

"Captain Cooper sends his thanks," Graham said, even though everyone on the bridge knew that Coop had done no such thing. Someone on his staff had. If Coop had done so, he would have spoken on all channels, just like he had a moment ago.

"We need other front line check-in," Sabin said. Technically, she wasn't the senior captain for all the front line ships on this shift, but no one took front line seriously during a respite period. Everyone had dinners and relaxation scheduled. Most bridges, even in the front line ships, were minimally staffed.

The only difference between a minimal staff in a front line ship and the other ships during a respite period was that the front line ships had top-notch crews manning the bridge, in case something did go wrong.

"Already done, sir," Graham said. "The captains are reporting to their bridges."

"What about our crew?" she asked. She felt almost embarrassed to ask. Graham was one of her most efficient crew members and she knew he had most likely pinged the bridge crew.

But she had to make sure—even in this respite period—that the crew was following protocol.

"Notified, and on the way," Graham said.

"Good, thank you." She sat in the captain's chair, and winced as the bow on the dress's back dug into her spine. A bow. What had she been thinking?

She knew what. The dress's tasteful blue fabric and demur front had caught her eye. But she had loved that bow for its suggestion of girlishness, something she wasn't now and would never be.

"Let's hear the check-in," she said.

Graham put the captains' responses overhead. In addition to the arrivals—all twenty of them—the captains seemed to believe it important to engage in a discussion of Coop's motives. A request for support was the lowest level request a captain could issue.

Normally, a captain in distress asked for a battalion of a particular type, not a general support request of warships.

So it was curious, but it spoke more to Coop's conservatism than to the situation at hand. Besides, no one seemed to acknowledge that the *Ivoire* had gone to Ukhanda at the request of one of its nineteen cultures. The Fleet had agreed to broker a peace deal between the Xenth and the Quurzod, but didn't know enough about either to do a creditable job.

The *Ivoire*, which had the best linguists in the Fleet, had gone into Quurzod territory to learn more about that culture in advance of the actual peace conference three months away. The *Alta*, the Fleet's flagship, apparently believed that the Fleet knew enough about the Xenth to do more limited preparation.

It had only been a month since the *Ivoire* had sent a team to the Quurzod. Apparently things had not gone well.

She shifted, the dress's shiny fabric squeaking against the chair's seat. She wasn't sure she had ever sat in her chair without wearing regulation clothing—at least, since she had become captain. As a little girl, she used to sit in her father's captain's chair on the *Sikkerhet*. This dress made her feel that young and that out of place.

Stupid chatter from the other captains surrounded her. They were still speculating on what Coop wanted and whether or not this was a legitimate request. They hadn't made the transition from respite to action. And there was another issue. Coop's message was low-key.

Only people who knew him well understood that he was worried.

"Open a channel," she said, unable to take the chatter any longer.

Graham nodded. Then he signaled her.

"Coop's asked for support," Sabin said in her most commanding voice. "Stop arguing about why, and haul your asses out there."

The chatter stopped immediately. She had a hunch she knew how the other captains had reacted: a straightening of the shoulders, a nod, a deep breath as they all gathered themselves, a momentary flush of embarrassment as they realized they had conducted themselves like people on vacation instead of captains on a mission.

She didn't like respite periods, so she didn't understand the vacation mindset. But a lot of these captains believed in relaxation, and believed the crap that the civilians on the various ships peddled, that a rested crew was a healthy crew.

She believed a practiced crew was an efficient crew.

She followed regulations, gave her staff the proper amount of time off, and no more.

Because this respite period was so long—months, really, as the Fleet prepared for the work around Ukhanda—she had her first officer, Charlie Wilmot, continually run drills. Each department had to run drills as well.

Her crew was going to remain the most disciplined crew in the Fleet. If a member of the crew complained, that crew member got transferred. Often, she'd trade that crew member for someone else on a different ship. She'd stolen more good officers from other ships than any other captain. The good officers, she believed, were the ones who wanted to work, not party at every opportunity.

Wilmot had just arrived on the bridge. His uniform looked crisp and sharp. He glanced at her dress and his lips turned upward just enough to register as a smile to anyone who knew him. Fortunately, no one else on the bridge watched him.

"The *Ivoire*'s in trouble," she said to him. "Graham will catch you up."

Wilmot nodded, then walked to his station not too far from hers. As he did, he looked up at the screen, frowned, and glanced at her again. But he didn't ask anything, because she had already told him to figure out what was happening from Graham.

As if Graham knew. No one on the bridge did, and it was clear that no one on the other front line ships did either.

She tapped the right arm of her chair, bringing up the captain's holographic console. She'd designed this so she didn't have to move to another part of the bridge to get information.

Before she'd followed the captain's training route, she'd started in engineering. While she loved design, she hated the lack of control the engineering department had. Plus, she was a captain's daughter, and she had ideas from the start on the way a well-run ship worked.

Most of the ships she had served on were not well run. So she had gone back to school, and had risen through the ranks until she got the *Geneva*. That was fifteen years ago. Even though she occasionally designed upgrades for her baby—upgrades that other engineers eventually brought to their ships—she hadn't really looked back.

She preferred being in charge.

Which was why, as the five other members of her team took their places on the bridge, she looked up those small, feather-shaped ships herself.

The ships weren't in the database, no matter how she searched for them. She searched by the ships' image, the design, and the area's history. She also searched through the images of Ukhandan ships, not that there were uniform ships on a planet that housed so many different cultures. Not all nineteen cultures were space-faring, but five of them were, according to the database, and those five had no ships like this.

Small, efficient, and capable of swarming.

She wanted to contact Coop, but she would wait. He would let her—and the other front line ships—know if something had changed.

She almost closed the console, when something caught her eye. She had images of the ships for five cultures, but the information before her contradicted itself. Five cultures had ships, but six cultures had gone into the space around Ukhanda.

The sixth culture, the Quurzod, were the ones that the *Ivoire* had gone to Ukhanda to study before the peace talks.

Her stomach clenched.

Clearly, something had gone very, very wrong.

"How far out are we?" Sabin asked Lieutenant Ernestine Alvarez, who was running navigation.

"Even at top speed, we're half a day away," Alvarez said.

Too close to use the *anacapa* drive with any accuracy. The *anacapa* was the thing that enabled the Fleet to negotiate long distances. It put a ship in foldspace, and then the ship would reappear at set coordinates. The problem was that the ship would reappear blind, and in a battle situation, that wasn't optimum.

Plus, time worked differently in foldspace, and while the best crews could predict the time differences down to the second, sometimes even the work of the best crews went haywire. Engineers claimed the problem was with sections of foldspace itself; scientists believed the problem was with certain *anacapa* drives.

Even with centuries of study and upgrades, neither group could come to a complete agreement. In Sabin's opinion, the Fleet had forever messed with something it did not understand when it started using the *anacapa* drive.

She wasn't going to use it on something like this. Nor was she going to order the rest of the front line to do so—not unless Coop sent out a major distress signal, which he had not yet done.

She wasn't going to explain herself to her crew, but if she had to, she would tell them what she always told them—that portion of the truth that they needed to know. It was the same truth every time they considered using the *anacapa* drive. The *anacapa* put a strain on the ship and on the crew that Sabin couldn't quite quantify. She hated using it for that very reason, just like most of the captains did.

Which was probably why Coop hadn't used his drive yet. The *anacapa* also worked as a shield. The ship would jump to foldspace for a moment, and then return to its original coordinates. Depending on how the *anacapa* was programmed, the return could happen seconds later or days later, without much time passing on the ship at all.

"Another twenty-five ships have just left Ukhanda's orbit," Alvarez said.

"That settles where the ships are from, at least," Graham said.

"It was pretty obvious that the ships were from Ukhanda," Phan said. "The question is which culture controls them."

That *was* the question. It would have an impact on everything: how the front line ships would proceed, how they would fight back, *if* they would do more than simply rescue the *Ivoire*. If they needed to rescue the *Ivoire*. Coop might get away on his own.

Sabin hoped Coop would get away on his own.

She asked Graham, "Have you sent a message to the *Alta*, asking if they know which culture owns these ships? Because we need to get some diplomats on the mission here, to ensure we don't make things worse."

The *Alta* was twice as large as all of the other ships in the Fleet, including the warships, and it housed the Fleet's government when that government was in session.

"I notified them as soon as we got Captain Cooper's message," Graham said. "I trust that they're monitoring the *Ivoire* as well."

Sabin was about to remind Graham that one should never "trust" someone else to do anything important, when Wilmot snapped, "Don't make assumptions, Lieutenant."

He sounded a bit harsh, even for him. Sabin glanced at him. That small smile had disappeared, and she saw, for the first time, how tired he looked. She wondered what he'd been doing during respite, besides running drills.

His uniform was so crisp she knew he had put it on right after the call to the bridge. So he'd been either asleep or doing something else when the call came in.

"Sorry, sir," Graham said, sounding just a bit contrite.

"I want identification on those ships," Sabin said. "We have time—half a day, you said. So let's see if we can cut that time short, and see if we can figure out who or what we're dealing with. The other cultures on Ukhanda are a mystery to me. Maybe they developed some technology of their own that we're not familiar with."

"Do you want me to send for Sector Research?" Meri Ebedat spoke up for the first time. She usually handled navigation, but she'd been doing some maintenance on the secure areas of the bridge during the respite period. She had a streak of something dark running along her left cheek, and her eyes were red-rimmed. Her brown hair had fallen from its usually neat bun.

She had to be near the end of her shift, although now, she wouldn't be leaving. She was a good all-around bridge crew member, and Sabin would need her as the mission continued.

"Yeah, do it," Sabin said, "although I doubt Sector Research knows much more than we do. We haven't had enough time to study Ukhanda. That was one reason the *Ivoire* was there."

"You think they did something wrong?" Wilmot asked her softly, but the entire bridge crew heard.

She knew what he meant: he meant had the *Ivoire* offended one of the cultures in a severe way.

But she gave the standard answer. "By our laws, probably not," she said.

He gave her a sideways look. He wanted a real answer, even though he knew the real answer. They all knew the real answer.

Had the *Ivoire*—or, rather, its on-planet team—offended one of the cultures? Clearly. And if Coop didn't act quickly, the entire ship might pay the price.

2

"Do you ever question it?" Coop asked Sabin months before, his hands behind his head, pillows pushed to the side, strands of his black hair stuck to his sweat-covered forehead.

They were in a suite on Starbase Kappa. They had pooled their vacation funds for the nicest room on the base—or at least, the nicest room available to someone of a captain's rank. Sabin hadn't stayed anywhere this luxurious in her entire life—soft sheets, a perfect bed, a fully stocked kitchen with a direct link to the base's best restaurant, and all the entertainment the Fleet owned plus some from the nearby sector, not that she had needed entertainment. She had Coop.

The two of them weren't a couple, not really. They were a convenience.

It was almost impossible for captains to have an intimate relationship with anyone once they were given a ship. Coop's marriage to his chief linguist—a marriage that began when they were still in school—hadn't made it through his first year as captain.

Sabin had never been married, and she hadn't been in love in decades. At least that was what she told herself. Because the people she interacted with on a daily basis were all under her command. She didn't dare fall in love with them or favor them in any way.

It wasn't against Fleet policy to marry or even sleep with a crew member (provided both had enough years and seniority to understand the relationship, and provided both had signed off with all the various legal and ethical departments), but it didn't feel right to her to sleep with and then command another person.

It didn't feel right to Coop either. They'd discussed it one night, decided they were attracted enough to occasionally scratch an itch, and somehow the entire convenience had improved their friendship rather than harmed it (as they had both feared it might).

Ever since, they would communicate on a private link between their ships, and when their ships had a mutual respite period, they got a room and scratched that itch, sometimes repeatedly.

She had been about to get out of bed and order some food when Coop spoke. She had the covers pulled back, but his tone caught her, and she lay back down.

"Do I question what?" she asked, grabbing one of his pillows and propping it under her back.

"Our mission," he said. "Or at least part of our mission."

She felt cold despite the blankets and the perfect environmental setting. She hadn't heard anyone question the Fleet's mission since boarding school. At that point, everyone questioned, just a little. They were encouraged to.

"You don't believe in the mission anymore?" she asked, turning on her side to face him. If Jonathon "Coop" Cooper no longer believed in the Fleet, well, then the Fleet might as well disband. Because the universe had shifted somehow and the rules no longer applied.

"Part of it," he said. "Although to say that I don't believe might be too strong. Let's just say I'm worrying about things."

He didn't look at her. He was staring at the ceiling, which was covered with a star field she didn't recognize. Starbase Kappa was old, built by her grandfather's generation and much of the base paid homage to places the Fleet had been almost a century ago. The Fleet usually liked to leave its past behind. Even the feats of bravery and the victories (large and small) became the stuff of legend, not something that the old-timers discussed as if they were meaningful events.

"What are you worrying about?" She propped herself up on her elbow so that she was in his field of vision.

He glanced at her, then smiled almost dismissively, and looked back up at the ceiling.

"What makes us so smart?" he asked.

She blinked, not expecting that.

"You and me?" she asked, thinking about their captains' duties.

He sat up, shaking his head as he did so. The blanket slid down his torso, revealing the dusting of black hair that covered his chest and narrowed on its way down his stomach.

Normally that would have distracted her, but his mood changed everything. She wasn't sure she had ever seen Coop this focused, even though she knew he was capable of it.

"Not you and me," he said. "The Fleet. We've been traveling for thousands of years. We go into a sector and if someone asks for help—or hell, if we figure they *need* help even if they don't ask—we give them assistance. We advise them, we make them see our point of view. We give them whatever they need from diplomatic support to military backup, and we stay as long as they need us, or at least until we believe they'll be just fine."

She'd been in hundreds of these kinds of conversations throughout her life, but never with another full adult vested with the powers of the Fleet. Always with children or teenagers or discontented civilians who traveled on the various ships.

Never with another captain.

"We never go back and check, we have no idea if we've done harm or good." Coop ran a hand through his hair, making it stand on end. "We continually move forward, believing in our own power, and we never test it."

"We test it," she said. "The fact that we've existed this long is a test in and of itself. We've been the Fleet for thousands of years. We've lived this way forever. We know the history of various regions. That's just not normal, at least for human beings."

"Because we never stick around long enough to be challenged," he said. "And we 'weed' out the bad elements, giving them crappy—and sometimes deadly—assignments or we leave them planetside someplace where we convince ourselves they'll be happy."

Her breath caught. Finally, a glimmer of what might have caused this mood.

"Did you have to leave someone behind, Coop?" she asked softly.

"*No*," he said emphatically, then gave her a look that, for a moment, seemed filled with betrayal. "Haven't you wondered these things?"

She hadn't. She wasn't that political. She stayed away from the diplomats and the linguists and the sector researchers. She didn't like intership politics or the mechanics of leadership.

She knew what she needed to know to run her ship better than anyone else in the Fleet—better than Coop, although she would never tell him that—and she left the rest to the intellectuals and the restless minds.

She had never expected such questioning from Coop. If anything, she found it a bit disappointing. She didn't want him to doubt the mission.

She had thought better of him than that.

She wasn't sure how to respond, because anything she said would probably shut him down. It might even interfere with the comfortable convenience of their relationship.

But he expected an answer. More than that, he seemed to need one.

"In my captaincy," she said after a moment, after giving herself some time to think, "the *Geneva* has never had an on-planet assignment. We've been front line or support crew or the occasional battleship. We don't get the diplomatic missions."

"You haven't thought about what we do, then," he said flatly.

"Not since school, Coop," she said, finally deciding on honesty.

"Not once? This mission from God or whatever is causing us to move ever forward, spreading the gospel of—what? A culture that we've never lived in and we no longer know existed?"

He sounded wounded, as if all of this were personal. She had to think just to remember what he was talking about. The Fleet left Earth thousands of years ago, and supposedly did have a mission, to find new cultures and to help them or something like that.

She had never paid attention to mythology and history in school. She didn't think it pertained to anything she was doing.

She still didn't.

"I think," she said gently, "we have our own culture now. The Fleet doesn't live on planets or moons. Its world is the ships. That's what we are. The ships. And everything else is what we do to maintain our ships. We do explore, we do encounter other peoples, but that's not the Fleet's main job. The Fleet's main job is to maintain the Fleet."

He slouched in the bed. "Oh, hell, that's even more depressing."

"Why do you question?" she asked.

He gave her that betrayed look again, then threw the covers back.

"Why do you breathe?" he asked, and left the room.

3

"Captain," Graham said, "I managed to modify our visuals just a bit. Those little ships *are* firing."

Sabin stood so that she could see the screen better. She had assumed that the little ships were doing something to the *Ivoire*, but, she realized as she watched, she hadn't thought of it as *firing* on the larger ship for two reasons.

The first reason was that something that small couldn't have weapons that would damage the *Ivoire*—not individually, anyway, and to her, somehow, that meant that any shots those little ships did take would be harmless. The second reason she hadn't thought the little ships were firing was that the *Ivoire* didn't seem to be reacting as if it were being shot at.

Why wasn't Coop shooting back? He could blow those things apart.

But the modified view showed little rays of light, coming from the small ships and hitting the *Ivoire* with a flare. The light and the flare were clearly constructs that Graham had designed to make the shots visible.

Still, they seemed creepy and a little overwhelming, rather like being stung continually by tiny insects. Pinpricks in isolation were annoying. Continual pinpricks weren't just annoying, they became painful.

"Have those ships been targeting more than one area on the *Ivoire*?" she asked. The answer wasn't readily apparent from the images that Graham had designed.

"I don't know," he said, "but if they are, the *Ivoire's* in real trouble. From what I can tell, those ships have a lot of firepower."

The weapons she understood, the ones that worked against great ships like these, required a lot of space and often their own power system away from the ship's engines. She had never seen ships so tiny with repeated firepower, the kind that could do damage on something like the *Ivoire*.

That wasn't entirely true. It was possible, if the ships gave up something, like speed. But these little ships kept up with the *Ivoire* and had powerful weapons.

"How is that possible?" she asked.

"I don't know," Graham said. "They're not like anything we've ever encountered before."

"And," Phan said, "they don't seem to be anything our various allies have encountered either."

"What about the Xenth?" Sabin asked. The Xenth weren't really allies, but they were the ones who suggested the brokered peace conference.

"I'm not getting anything from Sector Research," Phan said. "They're scrambling for information from the *Alta*. But they're not finding anything."

"Which might mean that there's nothing to find," Wilmot said.

He seemed unusually pessimistic. Sabin frowned at him. He didn't look at her. He was bent over his console, working furiously on improving their speed so that they could get to Coop faster.

"Captain." The single word cut through all the discussion. It was Alvarez. "Look at the *Ivoire*."

Sabin looked. It seemed to glow.

"Is that your effect, Perry?" she asked Graham.

"No, sir," he said. "That's the *Ivoire*."

Sabin had never seen anything like that before. "What the hell is that?"

The *Ivoire's* glow increased and then the ship vanished.

"Tell me they activated their *anacapa*," she said, hoping she didn't sound as worried as she felt.

"They did," Graham said, "but I only know that because I just got a transmission from them a few minutes ago, announcing their intention to do so."

"That transmission should be simultaneous with the *anacapa's* activation," Sabin said. "We should have gotten it as the *Ivoire* vanished."

"Yes, sir," Graham said, his tone speaking to the problem more than his words did.

"Keep this screen open, but show me what happened when that transmission was sent," she said.

Another screen appeared next to the main screen. On it, the ships—all of them, including the *Ivoire*—were in slightly different positions.

The little rays of light kept hitting the *Ivoire* in various places all over its hull.

"Dammit," Ebedat said.

"What?" Sabin said. She hadn't seen anything. But her eye kept getting drawn to the scrum of little ships left in the *Ivoire*'s wake. The *Ivoire*'s disappearance seemed to have confused them. Or maybe they were automatic, and unable to cope with a target that suddenly vanished.

"I think," Ebedat said, "and let's put an emphasis on 'think,' okay? I *think* that six shots hit the *Ivoire* as it activated the *anacapa*."

"That shouldn't cause a problem," Wilmot said.

"Not with weapons we understand," Ebedat said, "but these didn't show up on our system without some tweaking from Lieutenant Graham."

"Good point," Sabin said, wanting to shut down dissent while Ebedat had the floor.

"And look." Ebedat froze the frame, then went over to it and pointed. "Three of those shots hit the general vicinity of the *anacapa* drive."

"The most protected drive on all the ships," Wilmot said. "You can't hit the *anacapa* without penetrating the hull."

"Do we have proof that the hull was penetrated?" Alvarez asked.

"There's no obvious damage," Graham said.

Sabin frowned at it all. "We don't know what kind of weapons they're using. They might have penetrated the hull without damaging it."

"That's not possible," Wilmot said.

"Most cultures would say the *anacapa* isn't possible either," Sabin said, "and almost everyone we've encountered hasn't figured out that foldspace exists."

The bridge was silent for a moment. The second screen's image remained frozen. On the first screen, the little ships swarmed the spot where the *Ivoire* had been, almost as if they were trying to prove to themselves that it hadn't become invisible.

"The *anacapa* couldn't have malfunctioned and created that light," Wilmot said, but he didn't sound convinced.

"We don't know if that light came from the weapons," Sabin said. "The *Ivoire* is probably in foldspace right now. Did Captain Cooper send us a window? How long does he plan to be in foldspace?"

"That part of the message was garbled," Graham said. "Give me a moment to clean it up."

"How long would you remain in foldspace, Captain, if this were happening to the *Geneva?*" Phan asked.

"The *Ivoire* knew support was half a day out," Sabin said. "That would seem like a blip in foldspace. They could return without worrying about the little ships."

She hoped that was what Coop had done. Just because one captain would do it didn't mean another would. It was logical, though. And then they could all take on the problems caused by those little ships.

"They'll also get a chance to assess damage," Wilmot said, "and maybe recalibrate their own weapons to take out those little ships."

Sabin frowned. Coop hadn't fired on those ships, that she had seen anyway. Maybe he had other reasons that he couldn't do so. Maybe his weapons systems weren't working. Maybe he already knew that the weapons had no effect on those little vessels.

"He planned a twenty-hour window, sir," Graham said. "At least I think that's what the *Ivoire's* message said. I'm coordinating with several others in the front line. We'll let you know if that estimate is wrong."

"It sounds right to me," Sabin said. "It gives the *Ivoire* enough time to do some work on its own and it gives those small ships enough time to give up on the *Ivoire* and think it gone."

"And it also gives enough time for us to arrive," Wilmot said.

"Is he leaving this mess for us to clean up?" Phan asked, a bit too bluntly.

But Sabin knew what she meant. "The Fleet is operating diplomatically on Ukhanda. Once fire is exchanged, diplomacy ends."

"Yeah, so why wouldn't we fire?" Phan asked.

"I mean, once *we* fire, diplomacy ends," Sabin said.

"So we're supposed to take it when someone shoots at us?" Phan asked.

Had Phan never been in a battle? Sabin couldn't remember. It had been a long time since the *Geneva* had been under fire.

"Sometimes," Sabin said. "But we're generally not a diplomatic ship. Captain Cooper's weapon components would be different for this mission, and his orders would be constrained."

"Twenty hours," Wilmot said, clearly wanting to change the conversation. Protecting Phan? Sabin couldn't tell. "Does he want us there early to take the action he couldn't take?"

"He probably wants the show of force," Graham said. "It's one thing for a bunch of tiny ships to go after a large ship. It's another to face twenty ships from our front line."

Graham had a point. And Sabin had a job to do. She had to get her ship to that location, but she also needed clear instructions from the *Alta*. The diplomatic mission might be important or it might be something that the front line could scrub.

"I'm going to change," Sabin said, "and while I'm in my cabin, I'm going to see if I can get clear orders from the *Alta* on what we need to do when we get to Ukhanda. The last thing we need to do is blunder our way into a crisis."

Phan looked at her, expression serious. This time, however, Phan didn't say anything.

Wilmot was still staring at the screen as if he were trying to understand it.

"For the moment, Charlie," Sabin said to him, "you have the comm. Notify me if anything changes. And do your best to get us to that spot as fast as we can go, would you?"

"Yes, sir," Wilmot said.

She tugged on her bracelet as she left the bridge. To tell the truth, she was relieved that the dinner wouldn't happen. She liked action. She liked doing her job, not talking about trivial things.

She was worried about Coop, but he could take care of himself.

Her most important job now was to make sure the *Geneva* didn't screw up the Fleet's plans for the region.

She needed guidance, and she needed it now.

4

IT ONLY TOOK SABIN A FEW MINUTES TO REMOVE THE DRESS and put on her uniform. Her uniform felt like a second skin to her. She glanced at the bed, her dress with its bow and fancy fabric splayed on top of the coverlet and wondered what she had been thinking. She expected her crew to be prepared on the front line.

She should have been too.

Her quarters were the largest on the *Geneva*, not because she reserved the best for herself, but because regulations insisted. She had to put up with a certain amount of ceremony as captain, and she didn't like it any more than she liked the dress.

But she appreciated her quarters this evening. Because, unbeknownst to most of the crew, the captain's quarters had a backup control area, along with its own private communication network. And to get into that area took several layers of identification and approval. Once she was inside—alone—no one else could get in without even more identification and approval from her.

The area was just off her bedroom. A panel in the wall hid the entrance to the backup control area.

She finger-combed her hair, then went through the various protocols that opened the panel. It slid back, revealing a small space that looked more elaborate than the backup controls in engineering. In addition to the backup navigation, piloting, and weaponry, there was an entire console for communications.

She closed the panel, then settled in, facing the communications console. This was where she had usually contacted Coop. In fact, he was the person she spoke to the most from this room.

It felt odd not to contact him at all.

The thought made her just a little shaky. She wasn't sure why she was so on edge about his message, even though her counselor at the academy would tell her why she was. He would have said that it had to do with her father.

Sabin set that aside.

She took a deep breath, feeling the calm she was known for descending on her.

She put a message through to Command Operations on board the *Alta*. Command Operations guided the Fleet. It was an organization of top-ranked officials, most of whom had served with distinction as captains of their ships once upon a time. They were the ones who essentially ran the Fleet.

There was a civilian government, but because the Fleet's origins were military, the power structure remained so. The civilian government took care of general management and often took care of diplomatic relations, but in situations like this one, Command Operations took charge.

Sabin identified herself, and then she said, "I realize I'm not senior captain for the front line, but so far, the senior captain hasn't checked in."

And she hoped that message got through: the front line's senior captain was so far away from his duties that he couldn't come to a support request in a timely fashion.

"We're heading toward the *Ivoire's* position as per Captain Cooper's request. We'll be there in less than twelve hours. But we all have some questions about the mission."

Finally the screen across from her winked on, revealing the faces of several members of Command Operations. She had met two of them, including General Zeller who had been the first to question her abilities to captain, more than twenty years ago. The other three faces looked familiar, of course, and even if she hadn't known them by reputation, the listing of names and credentials below their images would have helped her understand who she was talking to.

The faces seemed to float against a black background. Long ago, Command Operations had established its communications imagery to show only the pertinent information and nothing more. In conversation with a captain, only the faces had been deemed pertinent.

"Your mission or Captain Cooper's?" asked General Nawoki, the other person that Sabin had met personally. She barely knew General Nawoki, although she admired

Nawoki's military record. Nawoki was one of the few officers who had defended her ship—with no loss of life—in a four-day prolonged battle after her *anacapa* had broken down. At one point, overrun by the enemy, she managed to stave off boarding and ship capture by reengineering half of the lifepods into weapons.

"I'm interested in both missions," Sabin said. "According to what little we saw of the attack, Captain Cooper did not fire on the ships. Speculation from our Sector Research team is that these ships are Quurzod, and we know that the *Ivoire* was on a pre-diplomatic mission to the Quurzod. I need to know—the entire front line needs to know—if we're not to fire on those ships, or if the diplomatic mission is off."

The members of Command Operations did not look at each other—that she could tell, anyway. She had no idea how the cameras were set up in Command Operations. She didn't even have a high enough rank to enter the level on the *Alta* that housed Command Operations, let alone ever go into the room.

"Anything else?" Nawoki asked.

"When we arrive," Sabin said, "who runs the mission? The front line commander or Captain Cooper?"

"Why do you care now?" Zeller asked.

Sabin glanced at him. His face had more lines than it had when she was in school, but his eyes remained the same. Steel gray, flat, and cold. She had tried not to hate him back then. Given the resentment she felt now as she looked at him, she wondered if she had been successful.

"It will make a difference as to how we plan our response. A cursory study of the ships on front line tells me that none of us have the kind of diplomatic experience that the crew of the *Ivoire* have, and if this is still a diplomatic mission, then—"

"We will get back to you," Nawoki said, and the images vanished from the screen. The contact had been severed.

Sabin stood and let herself out of the room, leaving the panel open in case Command Operations responded immediately. She didn't want anything to record the expression that she had barely been able to keep off her face inside that room.

She knew why Zeller had asked her why she cared now. The bastard thought she was panicking. Even after fifteen years of exemplary command, he thought some ship slipping into foldspace made her panic.

Then she let out a long breath. Maybe she was misjudging him. Maybe the problem was something else entirely, a diplomatic problem that no one in Command Operations could discuss in front of her.

She stretched, trying to relax her muscles, and willed herself to focus on the moment.

The past did not matter, whether it was her past relationship with General Zeller or the disappearance of her father.

What mattered was this mission, and how she would handle it. How her crew would handle it. How the front line would handle it.

And whether or not they would imperil a diplomatic mission.

And if anyone in Command Operations asked her about her reasons for asking questions, she would not be defensive. She would answer honestly. She would tell them she wanted to do what was best for the Fleet.

Because she did.

5

Her first encounter with George Zeller had come more than two decades before, when he was still a major. He reluctantly ran the counselors in the evaluation section of the academy's officer training program and, she later learned, he had taken no interest in the psychological evaluations or their necessity until she enrolled.

Correction: until she enrolled and did well.

Then, apparently, Major George Zeller made it his business to prove that she wasn't fit to command anything larger than an engineering staff on a third-class Fleet vessel.

He had been younger then, not just in age or experience, but in manner. He had red hair and green eyes that flashed when he was angry, which to her, seemed like all of the time.

He was the one who mentioned her father's disappearance to the academy staff, he was the one who believed that disappearance would cause problems, and he was the one who insisted on psychological training so rigorous that Sabin had to go without sleep for days to complete the testing and her schoolwork. When she complained to the head of her department, he moved the testing to dates between the school terms, enabling her to at least get some rest.

She always tested well, but Zeller kept accusing her of gaming the system. She finally reported him to his superior, one Colonel Gaines who would eventually disappear himself in an *anacapa* accident two years later. She never quite got over the irony of that; Zeller never got over the fact that she went over his head.

He might have overcome it, had she failed in Officer Training, but she had graduated first in her class, with high honors, the only person in twenty years to get a perfect score on all of the final term tests—including the physical ones.

She never quite figured out what Zeller had against her; other students had lost parents to accidents, disappearances, and explosions, and Zeller had never taken an interest in them.

Just her.

It wasn't until years later, after she had become a captain, that she found a reference to Zeller in her father's file. The record itself was mostly redacted. What did exist was deliberately vague.

After that discovery, she told herself that Zeller's reactions to her came from survivor's guilt, but she never really wanted to test that theory. So she avoided him whenever possible.

In fact, she had avoided him for more than a decade. Until now.

6

A SOFT, ALMOST INAUDIBLE CHEEP LET SABIN KNOW THAT the screen had activated. She slipped back into her chair, letting the panel close behind her.

Only one face floated in the blackness—that of General Nawoki. She looked tired, but Sabin didn't know if that was her natural state.

"We are getting conflicting reports from Ukhanda," Nawoki said. "The Xenth claim that the Quurzod killed all but three of the team members the *Ivoire* sent to the Quurzod. The Quurzod claim that the *Ivoire's* team violated Quurzod law and declared war. Word from some of the other cultures on Ukhanda is that the Quurzod are quick to offend and even quicker to use violence to punish the offenders. Unfortunately, the *Ivoire* herself has not sent us their report on the incident, so we have no way to assess the truth of the interaction. In other words, hold back until the *Ivoire* returns from foldspace, and let Captain Cooper lead the response."

It sounded like a mess and reinforced to Sabin, yet again, that she wanted nothing to do with actual diplomatic missions.

"Captain Cooper said he would keep the *Ivoire* in foldspace for twenty hours. We'll arrive eight hours before he returns. Should we stay out of the area until we have word of the *Ivoire*?"

Nawoki's lips thinned. She glanced over her shoulder at someone or something that Sabin could not see. Either Nawoki disagreed with the command she was about to give, or she was giving that command over the disagreements of others.

Sabin had no way to know which was true, only that Nawoki seemed as uncomfortable about the situation as Sabin felt.

"If those small ships remain, then stay out of the area," Nawoki said.

"And if they show up after we enter the same area?"

"Try to ascertain whose ships they are. See if they will negotiate or explain their position."

Sabin's breath caught, and she had to struggle to hold back her initial reaction. She had hoped that Command Operations had known who those ships belonged to.

"Do we have any theories as to whom the ships belong?" she asked.

"The Xenth say they are Quurzod ships, but our other sources on Ukhanda cannot confirm," Nawoki said.

"And forgive me, sir, but why aren't we trusting the Xenth?"

"Because we are getting conflicting signals from them. They claim they want peace with the Quurzod, but they are building their own military. Our Sector Research Team is also locating some evidence that the breaches of previous agreements might have come at the instigation of the Xenth rather than through the general warlike nature of the Quurzod."

Coop's voice echoed in Sabin's mind: *Do you ever question it? Our mission. Or at least part of our mission. What makes us so smart?*

"Were we planning to broker on the side of the Xenth?" Sabin asked, feeling like Phan—naïve and a bit out of her depth, and hoping that the General wouldn't notice or would take pity and answer her.

"We believed we could bring peace to Ukhanda," Nawoki said primly.

What makes us so smart? The memory of Coop's voice floated through Sabin's mind. She had to concentrate to keep his doubts from infecting her.

"We believed, sir?" she asked.

"Something went wrong, Captain," Nawoki said. "And after we recover the *Ivoire*, we will figure out what that something was."

7

THE REST OF THE TRIP TO THE UKHANDAN PART OF THE sector was uneventful. Captain Seamus Cho of the *Bellator* finally took over his role as commander of the front line. He had, apparently, been holding a bachelor party for a crew member and hadn't heard the summons in all of the ruckus.

In Sabin's opinion, Cho did not seem concerned enough about the *Ivoire* or the situation near Ukhanda. But he was operating under the same orders that Sabin was, and so she knew he would at least wait, the way she would have, for the *Ivoire* to reappear.

Coop would be sensible, and he would know what to do.

As the front line approached an hour sooner than planned, the small ships remained, patrolling the area as if they expected the *Ivoire* to return.

Most ships with strong sensors left a fighting region shortly after a Fleet ship disappeared. The sensors would show that the Fleet ship had left somehow and was not cloaked. Even ships that had poor sensors would get the message after eleven hours.

Either these small ships knew how the Fleet used their *anacapa* drives or the commanders of those ships were extremely stubborn, holding that small region of space as proof that they had conquered it.

Cho ordered the entire front line to remain just outside of standard sensor range—close enough to join any fight should the *Ivoire* return suddenly, but far enough away for a battle to be a struggle for any ships with planetside bases.

Finally, after eighteen hours, the small ships gathered into a V-shaped pattern and headed back toward Ukhanda. The entire front line tracked them, but did not see the ships go back to a base on the planet. Instead, they went past Ukhanda toward a small satellite that looked like it was part of an uninhabited sister planet.

Cho should have sent a ship to investigate, but he didn't. He believed their mission was to rescue the *Ivoire*, not to pursue the *Ivoire's* attackers.

Sabin couldn't argue with him. She might have made the same call herself, had she had command of the front line. It seemed as if Cho was as leery of getting involved in any diplomatic incident as she had been.

Finally, thirty minutes from the twenty-hour mark, he ordered the front line to prepare to defend the *Ivoire*. The front line would move slowly forward, not enough to attract attention from Ukhanda, but enough to get them in better range of the *Ivoire*.

They had covered half the distance to the *Ivoire's* last location when twenty hours came.

And went.

No one panicked. The *anacapa* drive could be finicky, and all of the captains had miscommunicated or misestimated their time in foldspace at one point or another.

Twenty-one hours passed.

Then twenty-two.

And finally, the front line got nervous.

Cho gave the standard search orders. A standard three-dimensional search pattern should have used twenty-four ships, but the front line didn't have that many. Besides, a few had to remain in position, in case the *Ivoire* returned later.

Cho assigned sixteen ships to the grid search, and left three ships in a waiting position. The fourth ship would go to an area not too far from the *Ivoire's* return site—close enough to be a bit dangerous, but far enough to prevent most collisions from happening.

That ship would be the most vulnerable: if the *Ivoire* returned to slightly different coordinates and the other ship's failsafes did not work, the ships might collide. But it was a standard risk at this point in delayed *anacapa* response.

Cho contacted Sabin before making the assignment. He used a private channel so that the other ships couldn't hear their conversation, even though the bridge crew could.

He turned up on her screen, tall and stately in his uniform. He had zoomed out the image so that she could see his entire bridge crew, who looked as busy and focused as hers.

"I want to assign you to the on-site investigation spot," he said. "You have the most experience. However, General

Zeller told me that you might not want the task. I don't believe in taking one person's word for another's possible reaction, especially when the other person is available. You're the best person for the job, Tory. Do you want it?"

"Of course I do," she said, keeping her voice calm. The momentary flash of annoyance at Zeller's name and remark had already faded. Zeller was a problem for another day. "Do you want me to do a grid search or an area search?"

"See if you can find traces of the *Ivoire*," Cho said. "Barring that, see if you can figure out exactly what they did."

Something in his phrasing seemed strange to her.

"Don't you think they used their *anacapa* drive?" she asked.

"I do, but I've never seen one take so long to engage, and I've never seen a ship light up like that," he said. "I'm worried that they disappeared, not because of the *anacapa* but because those little ships used a weapon we don't understand."

Sabin felt chilled. She hadn't even thought of that possibility. In that case, Coop—and his entire crew—were already dead.

But she shouldn't guess. Guessing was the enemy in any search for information.

"If those ships used such a powerful weapon," she said, "why would they have remained in the area?"

"I don't know," Cho said. "I don't think they would have. But I can't rule out anything at the moment. We need to search."

She agreed. "I'll do my best to figure out what happened here," she said. "I'll let you know when we have news."

She had almost said *if we have news*, and had caught herself just in time. Normally, she wasn't a pessimist, but something was odd here, something she could feel but couldn't see.

She wasn't usually a gut commander. She liked facts and hard information. But she also knew that sometimes hard information took too much time to acquire and gut became important.

She hoped this wasn't one of those times.

8

ON THE DAY HER FATHER DISAPPEARED, THEY PULLED Tory Sabin out of class on the *Brazza* and took her to the observation deck. She always remembered it as "they" because try as she might, she couldn't remember who took her from class, how she got to the observation deck, how many people spoke to her along the way, or what anyone expected of her.

She was all of thirteen, precocious and opinionated, one month into her new school—a boarding school, which was unusual at her age. Boarding school for most students started when they qualified for the final four years of mandatory education. She tested way ahead of her peers, and so got assigned to a special school for children her age who were on a fast track.

Her father was proud of her. No one had bothered to tell her mother.

But someone had told her mother that Sabin (whom everyone called Tory back then) was alone on the *Brazza*, waiting for news of her father, because her mother swooped in as if she would rescue everyone.

Her mother always wore impractical flowing garments, the kind of thing that confirmed she wasn't, nor would she ever be, part of the Fleet's military structure. She was an artist who worked in fabric. Her art changed each time she visited a new culture or planet, so her work became quite collectible among a certain group in the Fleet. She couldn't replicate patterns or materials once she ran out of whatever she had purchased in her (actually, the Fleet's) travels, so her pieces became—of necessity—limited editions.

Tory hadn't seen her mother in more than six months, even though the ship her mother lived on, the *Krásný*, never left the Fleet on any kind of mission. Most of the Fleet's civilians ended up on the *Krásný*, partly because the military presence was smaller on that ship. The ship specialized in environments and environmental systems, and that included the interior design that kept the people on board all of the ships entertained, stimulated, and sane.

Her mother sat beside Tory on a bench in the center of the room, enveloping her in lavender perfume. The bench was built so that the occupant had a 360-degree view of the space outside. Plus the domed ceiling was clear so that she could see everything above her.

Tory wanted to slide away. Her mother's perfume was overwhelming, but more than that, her mother's golden gown was made of some kind of shiny but rough fabric, and just being near it made Tory itch.

"They don't understand the *anacapa*, you know," her mother said conversationally, as if they'd been talking all along. No hello, no hug, no how-have-you-been, or even a comforting he'll-be-all-right. Nothing. Straight into the old arguments, with Tory standing in for her father. "It's dangerous to use them, and your father promised, back when we married, that he never would—"

"Fortunately, you're divorced," Tory said and stood up, arms crossed. "He's overdue by five hours. That's all, Mom. You can go back to whatever thing you're designing. I won't be mad at you. *I'm* not worried. Daddy's good at his job."

Her mother stood, and this time, wrapped her arms around Tory. Tory thought of elbowing her mother hard and viciously so that her mother would never hug her again, then suppressed the response and squirmed out of her mother's embrace.

"They don't remove a child from school or contact her remaining parent because they think this is routine," her mother said—so not comfortingly.

"I'm smart enough to know that, Mother," Tory said.

"They think you need me."

"They're wrong." Tory stepped closer to the observation window. "Daddy will be just fine. The *Sikkerhet* will return, and he and I will get on with our lives. *Without you.*"

Her mother tilted her head just a little, a dismissive *you can't mean that* look she had used as long as Tory could remember.

"I divorced him, not you," her mother said.

"Funny," Tory said, "I couldn't tell."

"I contacted your father about a visitation schedule. He never responded," her mother said.

On purpose, Tory almost said but didn't. He wanted to see if Tory's mother would push the visitation, wanted to see if she would make contract, if she would hire a lawyer to enforce the terms of the shared custody.

Her mother had done none of those things. In fact, she hadn't even done what was on her schedule—a series of intership calls that were supposed to happen every Friday night. Instead, she'd send apologies, usually about work-related distractions, and finally, she stopped apologizing altogether.

Tory's father had been surprised; he had thought Tory's mother was a different person, maybe from the beginning. Tory attributed his blindness to both love and to the fact that he hadn't spent much time with his wife once he got on a career track. It was only after he kept finding Tory on her own, in the engineering and maintenance areas of the ship, at an age when the crew would report Tory's appearance (because it was dangerous) that he finally realized his family couldn't stay on the ship when he had an actual mission.

When he broke that news to Tory and her mother, her mother had shrugged and said they would move to the *Krásný*. Tory had burst into tears, begging to stay, and her father, for once, had listened. Not that he could have missed the campaign. Because others on the ship said that Tory shouldn't—couldn't—stay with her mother. Not and have actual parental care.

"What happened between you and Daddy isn't my business," Tory said. "I—"

"It is your business, darling," her mother said. "If your father had—"

"I don't want to discuss it. In fact, I don't want you here. Daddy will return, and I'll be fine, and even if I'm not fine, you're not the kind of person who can take care of anyone. If you don't leave right now, I will."

Her mother stared at her as if Tory had betrayed her.

"You need me right now," her mother said. "I thought you were smart. No one misses an *anacapa* window without a reason, a serious reason. In the history of the Fleet, those who miss the window by an hour or more usually do not return. You have a scientific brain. You should understand—"

"Shut up," Tory said, her hands balled into fists. "Shutupshutupshutup."

"Tory—"

Tory waved her hand at her mother, effectively silencing her. Then Tory shook her head, and ran for the door. Tory had no idea where she was going to go—if she went back to her room, her mother would find her—but she had to get away.

Just like she had to get away when she was a child.

And like she had when she was a child, she found herself heading toward engineering, the only place on any ship with concrete answers.

The only place she had ever felt safe.

9

Sabin's search found evidence that Coop had used the *anacapa* drive. Sabin was relieved and not relieved at the same time. In fact, she couldn't remember a moment when her emotions over one event had been so mixed.

The fact that he had used the *anacapa* proved that those small ships didn't have some kind of miracle weapon that destroyed the *Ivoire*. But the fact that he used the *anacapa* and wasn't back in the same spot at the time he had mentioned meant he was in trouble.

Sabin's mother had been right all those years ago: those who miss the window by an hour or more usually did not return.

Sabin sent the information to Cho and asked if he wanted her to contact all the sector bases still in operation. Sometimes a ship having trouble with its *anacapa* wouldn't show up in the spot it was supposed to; it would instead go immediately to the nearest sector base for repair.

The fail-safe also took ships to sector bases, usually the most active one. If the crisis had been really bad, no one at the base would have thought of contacting the front line—if, indeed, the base even knew that the front line had moved.

Cho promised to check, and after he did, he requested a private audience with her. He wanted to talk to her nowhere near her crew or his.

She didn't think that unusual. She thought it sad. Because she knew part of what he was going to say.

Her ship had a small communications area just off the bridge. She had built that as well, for moments just like this one. When she thought about it, she realized she had made major modifications to every single ship she had served on, and on none more than the *Geneva*.

She slipped inside the communications area. It was larger than the one in her cabin. Ten people could fit in here comfortably, even though, if she needed that many people to hear something, then they would usually go to the conference area or listen on the bridge.

The communications into this section of the ship were scrambled and encoded, more private than anything else on the *Geneva*.

Screens covered all the walls. Everything could become holographic if needed, but she never used that feature. The table in the middle of the room felt out of place. She didn't sit at it.

Instead, she leaned on it, and contacted Cho.

He showed up on the screen in front of her, in a room similar to her own. His ship had been redesigned after she made modifications to hers.

Cho looked tired. Some of that might have been because of the bachelor party and the change of focus, but some of it was a man trying to cope with hard news, news that upset him, news he wanted to treat dispassionately, even though it was impossible.

"You think they're dead," she said without introduction. She had almost said, *you think* he's *dead*, which was an insight into her own mind that she didn't want and she certainly didn't want Cho to hear.

Either she thought Coop was dead, or she feared it, or she cared about it too much. After all, there were more than 500 souls on that ship. She should care about all of them equally.

"What I think doesn't matter," Cho said, which was clearly his version of yes. "They haven't shown up at any of the active sector bases or starbases. The *Alta* tells me that experts have pinged the older sector bases, and there's been no activity, at least activity that has shown up in the logs. Experts tell me that they shouldn't have gone back to sector bases that the *Ivoire* hasn't used in the past twenty years, so that double-check was a long shot."

She knew that. No ship had shown up on old decommissioned sector bases unless that ship had used or visited the sector base some time in its recent history.

"The *Alta* wants us to do a few things," he said. "They want us to wait until the *Taidhleoir* arrives. That ship will handle the situation on Ukhanda."

The *Taidhleoir* was another ship that specialized in diplomatic missions. It wasn't as top of the line as the *Ivoire*, but it would do.

"They figured out then who the ships belonged to?" Sabin asked.

"The Xenth say that the ships are Quurzod, but the Quurzod aren't acknowledging anything, and apparently the *Alta* can't confirm. It's a mess, and they don't want us in the middle of the diplomatic part of the mess. The front line has to remain, though. The show of force is going to show everyone on Ukhanda that the Fleet isn't to be messed with."

"Even though someone probably thinks they successfully harmed one of our ships," she said, more to herself than to Cho.

"Even though," Cho said, in the tone that captains used when they didn't approve of the path their higher ups were taking. "They also want us to do some investigating along the trails left by the small ships and near that spot where the *Ivoire* lit up so oddly."

"I have been," Sabin said.

"Not for an indication of *anacapa* use, but to see if there are other energy signatures that we're unfamiliar with, or maybe even ones we are familiar with. In other words, they want our investigators to figure out what those ships were attacking the *Ivoire* with."

"Reverse engineer it?" she asked. She'd been part of teams that had done such things in the past. They were usually used in war situations, when one of the participants had developed a new weapon. "We can't just ask someone on Ukhanda or capture one of the ships?"

Cho visibly shrugged, and he looked away for a moment. When he glanced back at her, his dark eyes held sadness and something else. Frustration? She didn't know him well enough to be able to tell.

"They think something really bad happened on that planet," he said, "and they believe it's going to take some work to deal with it. Work we can't do in a time frame that will enable us to rescue the *Ivoire*."

If they could rescue the *Ivoire*. He didn't even have to add that part for her to hear it.

"You didn't have to tell me all of this in private," she said. "You know our bridge crews could have kept this quiet. What else is there?"

"I wanted you to make a choice. Not your crew, not the *Alta*. You." Now his gaze met hers, and she almost felt him in the room. He was scared. She rarely had that thought about other captains, and she had never seen such emotion from Cho. Not that he was showing much now. His mouth had thinned a bit. Anyone who didn't know him would have thought he was just a little more concerned than normal, a little preoccupied.

But she could feel it: He was scared.

Was he scared of her response? Or something else entirely?

"Here's the thing, Tory," he said, his tone confidential. "I talked to some of the generals directly. We all know that time is of the essence in tracking a lost ship in foldspace. But General Zeller wants us to wait until some of the foldspace investigative and rescue ships arrive. He doesn't trust you."

Of course he didn't. He hadn't from the moment he met her.

"Trust me to what?" she asked, although she had a hunch she knew.

"Search foldspace." Cho spoke tersely as if he wanted to get this part of the conversation over with. And as she was about to respond, he added, "I don't understand it, Tory. You're the one who developed the search method that we've used for the past thirty-five years. You're the one who understands it the best. I know you and Zeller have issues, and I assume it's none of my business—"

"He thinks I'm too emotional about this," she said. "And you know, on this one thing, he might be right."

10

OLDER THAN HER YEARS, BRILLIANT, AND OBSESSED. THAT was what Sabin's evaluations all said. She had hacked into them on the night before the very first test mission began.

Her years were all of twenty, too young to do much in the Fleet, but old enough to be considered an adult. She had already gone to two boarding schools. She had worked her way through some of the most difficult engineering degree programs in the Fleet, plus she had done some work with the Dhom, one of the more advanced cultures they were lucky enough to find two years ago.

The scientists there taught her things about dimensional theory that no one in the Fleet had contemplated before. After they heard the Dhom scientists, some of her professors postulated that the Fleet had lost a lot of its research into dimensional theory. The professors claimed that the *anacapa* drive couldn't have been developed without it.

Some of her professors were a little naïve, in Sabin's opinion anyway. She could have pointed to a dozen points in the history of science and technology, points she knew, where something got developed accidentally and no one quite knew how it worked.

Granted, however, such things rarely inspired confidence, and she didn't need to point out that there were parts of her theories that were just guesses as well. Guesses based on research, but as she could have pointed out to anyone who listened (as she would argue sometimes inside her own mind), theories needed testing before they became quantifiable.

Her test missions were the transition between theory and fact. Or at least, between narrower, more apt theories, and something approaching fact.

What she couldn't admit to anyone—not her mentors, not the professors, not the captains running the ships that would take these risks—was that she really didn't care about ancient history, *anacapa* development, or even dimensional theory.

She cared about finding her father and his crew.

And if her theories were right, then even now, she might find them, trapped in foldspace for only a few hours or days. Even if seven years had gone by for them, as those seven years had gone by for the Fleet, she might still discover some remnant of the ship. Maybe the *Sikkerhet* had gone to a nearby planet and settled. Maybe it had simply refueled and waited, trying to figure out how to return to what the Fleet called "real space," which was, the current space and time.

The one thing the Fleet had done was build a long-term future trajectory. The Fleet knew where it was going.

It was heading into what, for it, was uncharted space. It had advance ships to either map the area or to double-check the maps provided by the locals of the sector the Fleet was currently in.

The only thing uncertain in the Fleet's map was the timeline. The Fleet had none. It would spend months near some planet, learning the culture. It would spend years helping a new ally fight a war.

If her father knew the trajectory, he might be waiting for the Fleet *ahead* of where the Fleet currently was. She doubted that, though, since the *Alta* had sent large ships as well as exploratory vessels ahead, searching for the *Sikkerhet*.

If her father had gone too far into the trajectory, she might never see him again. The version of the Fleet that greeted him or the descendants on his ship might be populated by her grandchildren's generations—if, indeed, she ever had grandchildren.

The method she had devised, the method that ultimately got tested, was a three-part grid search inside foldspace. The Fleet had never done foldspace grid searches for lost ships before, not in all the millennia of its existence.

Part of that was a simple disagreement as to what foldspace was. Some theorists believed that foldspace was a different point in time—the future, the past—some*when* else. But a lot of the practical military, those who'd actually flown into foldspace through their *anacapa* drives, didn't believe that.

The star maps in foldspace were significantly different than the star maps from the area where the ship had left. It usually took something catastrophic to change star maps in the same area—not even the explosion of a planet would change a star map so drastically as to be completely unrecognizable.

So most theorists believed that foldspace was either an alternate reality that somehow the ships tapped into with the *anacapa* or a fold in space, an actual place that the ships could somehow access.

What Sabin privately believed was that the *anacapa* sent a ship far across the universe, into another galaxy altogether, and then back again. But the scientists told her that the *anacapa* didn't have the energy for that. Nothing did.

Which left her with dimensional theory. One of her professors claimed that foldspace was another dimension, one that hadn't yet been charted and wasn't understood. Some of the work done by the scientists on Dhom pointed to that theory being correct.

She had been contemplating all of that when she realized that none of it mattered. *What* the ships went into wasn't important. What it *seemed like* was.

And what it seemed like was a sector of space like all other sectors of space, except for the different star maps. Except for the fact that none of the equipment that the Fleet had could track the ships down in that sector of space. None of the equipment that any other culture had could track those ships either.

So she decided to do what all the scientists of the *anacapa* had done before her—not question how it did what it did—but accept the reality that it worked.

In that reality, the ships went somewhere that looked like this reality.

And those realities could be searched.

If she could find the right point in foldspace, the same entry point that a missing Fleet ship had taken.

The same entry point that the *Sikkerhet* had taken.

The same entry point that her father had taken—and disappeared.

11

"Oh, come on," Cho said in a tone she'd never heard him use before. "Zeller's unreasonable. Everyone knows that. They're just waiting for him to retire."

Sabin blinked at him, forcing herself to come back for a moment in her own past. A quick escape in her own mental foldspace.

The small control room was hot. She pushed a strand of hair off her face, and resisted the urge to smile grimly. Cho was staring at her with something like sympathy, which she would not have expected from him.

"I know they're waiting for him to retire," she said. "They think he's old-fashioned. But he's not entirely unreasonable."

Cho frowned. He looked like he was about to disagree, when she said, "He's lived through a lot, Seamus. Sometimes we don't respect that enough."

"I can't believe you're agreeing with him, after the way he treats you."

Her smile was thin. "Yeah, I know," she said. "But I think I don't treat him well either."

12

When Sabin was twenty-one, she hadn't known who Zeller was. He'd just been a crew member on the *Rannsaka*, one of the ships that had used her grid system to explore foldspace in search of her father's ship.

Zeller had simply been a face in the crowd when she boarded the *Rannsaka*, heading to its largest crew dining room for a briefing.

What she encountered was a celebration.

Over two hundred crew members applauded her as she walked into the room. The captain, a severe woman who until this point rarely seemed to smile, had led the cheers, then surprised Sabin by saying,

"And thanks to Tory Sabin, we now know what happened to five of our vessels. Five, considered lost, and now found."

Sabin's breath caught. She'd been running so-called test missions of the grid search for more than a year. The missions were no longer tests, really. Everyone knew they worked on some level. But so far none of the ships found had been the *Sikkerhet*. All had disappeared at different times, and in different sectors of space. None had had crew members that anyone knew, and indeed, the ships themselves had been empty for a long time. There weren't even bodies on board, although no one knew if the crews had left voluntarily or not. Most of the ships were open to space. Those ships could have been raided, abandoned, or simply suffered through the passage of time.

As of yet, no one had even tried those ships' *anacapa* drives or even tried to boot up the other equipment. The ships had piggybacked on the science vessels and had been taken to Sector Base T so that they could be studied.

Four of those ships anyway.

Sabin hadn't known about a fifth.

She turned to the captain and said softly, "There's a fifth?"

"Yes," the captain said with a smile. "We found it at the very end of our search and it's already at Sector Base T. And this one's mostly intact."

Sabin knew better than to ask the captain why no one had contacted Sabin. Gradually the mission was changing from testing to something run by the military, and the military rarely gave out information.

The entire crowd had grown silent. Maybe they saw Sabin's reaction, a tentative response, not quite the joy everyone had expected.

She had gotten the news on the other four in her command headquarters on the *Pasteur*, and she had been with her team. They knew she had been searching for one ship in particular, so her mixed reactions hadn't bothered them.

She wished she could remain as calm as a scientist should in such circumstances, but her heart rate increased. Her face was slightly flushed and she knew she looked just a bit too eager.

"What ship is it?" she asked, suspecting she knew the answer. After all, why would they throw a celebration if it weren't the *Sikkerhet*?

"The *Moline*," the captain said.

The ship's name rolled around in her head for a long moment. *Moline. Moline.* She hadn't even heard of that ship. She had heard of two of the others before they were found, but the *Moline* wasn't one that had any obvious known history.

She could feel her intellect trying to wrap itself around the news, while her heart sank. She needed to leave the room, she needed to be alone with this, but she also needed to acknowledge everyone's good work.

"That's excellent," she said and hoped she sounded enthusiastic.

"And," the captain said with that unbelievably cheerful sound in her voice, "I wanted to let you know that the *Alta* has decided that your foldspace searches are now going to become part of the Fleet's regular systems. We'll design ships to do the searches, train people, everything. Your program is official now!"

The crew cheered and applauded. Sabin smiled at them—at least, she hoped she smiled. How come no one had told her this personally? Why were they doing this kind of "celebration"? Didn't they know this wasn't about the old ships or even the program? It was about her father.

At the thought of him, the frustration she'd been holding back welled up. She knew better than to react here. Instead she smiled, waved some more, and then nodded once, fleeing the room.

She made it halfway down the corridor before she burst into tears. She had known things would change at some point, but she figured she'd find her father first.

The search wasn't refined enough yet. She couldn't pinpoint where a ship disappeared and where it had gone to in foldspace. The grid search had used *anacapa* signatures to track ships, yes, but they weren't ships that anyone had been searching for. They had disappeared long ago; their crews would have been dead now, anyway.

Some of the *Rannsaka*'s crew came through the corridor. She turned away, unable to go farther, and hid her face against the wall, hoping no one would stop for her.

One man did. He touched her back, asked if she was all right.

"Yes," she had lied. "Yes. Just tired."

She had no idea if she knew him or if he knew her. She never ever learned who he was. But later, she'd come to suspect Zeller. Zeller, who realized how broken up she had been over not finding her father's ship, about effectively being removed from running the program she had started.

Or maybe that man had been someone else, and she had given Zeller too much credit. Maybe the man—whoever he had been—had no memory of an incident that loomed so large in her own mind.

The next day, she asked to search for her father's ship. Her request was denied. Apparently Command Operations on the *Alta* wanted to examine the five recovered ships before searching for any more.

They told her to put in a request for a future search, and they would get back to her.

They commended her for her service. They designed an entire group of ships to search foldspace, based on her plans. They offered to promote her.

She let them.

And six months later, she was moved from foldspace search to engineering, where she was supposed to improve the *anacapa* design.

Five years after that, after applying and reapplying to search for her father's ship to no avail, she applied to the academy for officer training.

And, it turned out, only Zeller had figured out why.

13

"I HAVEN'T RUN A SEARCH SINCE THE VERY FIRST ONE, decades ago," Sabin said to Cho. "Things have changed, procedures have changed, and honestly, I haven't kept up with most of it."

She shifted in her chair. The room had closed in on her.

Cho nodded. "I glanced at the information, and from what I can tell, the only time we recovered a ship in fold-space right after the ship missed its window, we had gone in within twenty-four hours."

She closed her eyes. She could almost picture Coop, grinning at her over a private dinner in their suite on Starbase Kappa, teasing her about the changes in protocol on something or other. He had once told her that she jumped in too early, in his opinion, that a captain needed caution to protect his crew.

She had told him that a captain also had to know when to take a risk.

Cho said something, but she held up her hand to silence him. She needed a moment to think. He was going to explain risks to her that she understood, risks she invented for god's sake.

Ships had to dive in and out of foldspace just to do the grid search, and each trip into foldspace, each search, put the rescue ships at risk. The best grid search took the coordinated effort of five or more ships, exchanging information, going in, coming out, never staying in foldspace longer than a minute or two to gather information.

Because a minute or two in foldspace could be an hour or more outside of it.

Sixty minutes or sixty-five or sixty-three. The correlation was never entirely precise, which was what made foldspace so very dangerous.

In fact, there were three main things that made foldspace dangerous. The first was that no one entirely understood it, so the sensible captains were leery about using it. The second was that the sensors did not work between foldspace and real space. So returning from or going to foldspace meant that a ship might land on top of something else, like an asteroid or, in the case of real space, another ship.

And of course the final great risk was the one she dealt with right now: the longer a ship stayed in foldspace, the more unreliable the time of return became. No one could predict the exact moment the ship would come back, only that it would come within a time frame. That was why Coop said 20 hours, but he didn't specify down to the minute or second.

The biggest problem Sabin had now was this: the front line didn't have five ships to spare. She knew that, and

Cho hadn't mentioned any others. The crew of her ship was going to have to do something it wasn't trained for, and she would be risking her crew to save another.

Jumping in too fast.

She had a hunch Coop would have waited until the investigative team arrived.

She wouldn't.

She opened her eyes. Cho was watching her patiently, as if he expected her to say no. He had given her time, and she appreciated that, especially since his time was so valuable.

Just like hers was.

Like Coop's was.

"I think we need at least two ships to do this," she said. "And if there are crew members on any ship in the front line who used to work foldspace investigation and rescue, I'd like them to join my team for this rescue attempt."

Cho's jaw moved just a little, as if he started to say something and then held it back.

"The *Alta* didn't approve two ships for this," he said.

She started to argue, but it was his turn to hold up his hand.

"But," Cho said with great force. "I agree with you. If we're going to mount a rescue, we're going to do the best we can to get it right."

She grinned at him, and felt—astonishingly—a prickle of tears behind her eyes. Dammit, she cared more than she wanted to.

She probably should have admitted that as well, but she didn't. Besides, she suspected Cho understood.

She suspected his willingness to countermand the orders from the *Alta* had more to do with Coop and the *Ivoire* than it did any kind of common sense.

She appreciated it, but she didn't tell Cho that.

She suspected he already knew.

14

IT TOOK HALF AN HOUR TO PREPARE FOR THE RESCUE. The *Geneva's* partner ship on this mission was the *Pueblo*, commanded by Captain Jakoba Foucheux. Foucheux had spent two months in foldspace investigation and rescue before asking for a transfer. The reason for the transfer remained classified, a procedure that usually meant some issue with a superior officer, and usually one that never got properly resolved in any kind of arbitration.

Sabin didn't have any time to dig deeper. She was relieved to have Foucheux, whom she liked, as her partner, but disappointed that Cho had only found ten other crew members who'd worked in foldspace investigation and rescue. Of those ten, only five were available to transfer to Sabin's ship. The others were too far away on the search near Ukhanda to get back in time to start this mission.

The mission was deceptively simple. Once Sabin finished the math confirming what she believed Coop had done given the information he had given, the telemetry that the *Ivoire* had automatically sent to the Fleet, and given the time he'd been gone, she could—within a limited range —figure out the coordinates in foldspace.

The foldspace investigation and rescue section had a formula for all of this, and since they were the ones that had actually discovered recently missing ships in the past, she had two of the borrowed crew members use that formula as well.

All three people—the crew members and her, using her old system—had come up with the same location, which cheered her. If they had been searching for a ship that had disappeared long ago, they would have a lot more trouble coming up with the same location. They'd probably come up with three different locations, and maybe more, depending on how they all tweaked their formulas.

Once they had a location, the ships would work in tandem. First the *Geneva* would head to that part of foldspace and immediately scan the area. The *Geneva* would stay no more than a minute, and reappear, sending all of its scanned information to the *Pueblo*.

The *Pueblo* would do the same thing, scanning a slightly different swath of foldspace, and the two ships would continue to work in tandem until they found something, or until the actual investigation and rescue ships arrived.

The problem was that there were no guidelines on which direction to proceed once the searching ships moved beyond the scans of the original location. That was why five ships were better, and more than five desirable. The ships would partner, and go in *all* directions, doing so quickly, then moving to cover as much of that region of foldspace in the shortest amount of time.

Sabin had to pick a direction after the third set of tandem jumps, and she didn't like that. She hoped the *Ivoire* would be easy to find, that it would show up—even as a speck—on the nearest grid search. But she knew that hope and reality often failed to collide.

15

THE FIRST JUMP INTO FOLDSPACE FELT LIKE ANY OTHER. First, the thrum of the *anacapa* drive, which she barely heard or felt on a normal day, faded. Then the screens blanked. Sabin knew that if she were watching the navigation controls, they would flicker for just a moment.

The entire ship would bump, only once and very slightly. If she were in a vehicle on the ground, she would think that vehicle had hit a small rock, sending a tiny reverberation through the entire system.

Then the screens reappeared, the navigation controls clicked back full force, and that reverberation disappeared, replaced by the thrum of the *anacapa*.

Sabin had jumped into foldspace so many times, she usually didn't notice the details.

In fact, she could only remember noticing a few times in her past: on her first trip doing a grid search, on her first jump as chief engineer, and then the first time she piloted a vessel, as a lieutenant on the path to full command.

So, Sabin watched herself react here as if she were standing outside herself. Paying attention to those tiny details, common details, meant three things. She was worried about this grid search. She was worried about her ship.

And she was worried about Coop.

The images on the screen were a star map she didn't recognize. Even though that happened with every jump into foldspace, it was still something she noticed. She liked knowing exactly where she was, and in foldspace, she never did.

"Rapid grid search," she ordered, even though Wilmot, Phan, and Ebedat were already bent over their consoles. Sabin wanted to be in and out of foldspace as fast as she could.

"We have it, sir," Wilmot said.

"Good," Sabin said. "Let's go back."

Alvarez activated the *anacapa*.

As the screens blanked for the second time in less than a minute, Sabin said, "Graham, the millisecond we return, you need to send that information to the *Pueblo*. Even before we analyze."

"Yes, sir," Graham said.

By the time he finished speaking, the *Geneva* had returned to real space.

"Done, sir," Graham said, and as he spoke, the *Pueblo* vanished.

Sabin let out a small breath.

"Any ships?" she asked Wilmot.

"Not obviously in this first grid," he said. "How deep a search do you want?"

"It's all we got at the moment, so keep some part of the system probing as deep as possible," she said. "The better the search, the better our luck will be."

And as she said that, the *Pueblo* returned in the same place it had been a few minutes before.

"Okay," she said, "let's go again."

And they did.

16

Twenty-five searches later, Wilmot said, "Sir, the *Pueblo* may have found something."

Sabin's heart rose, but she made herself take a deep breath and tamp down the emotion. "May" was not definitive enough, and Foucheux was the kind of woman who would be accurate in her descriptions.

"Tell the *Pueblo* that we'll delay our search to see what's on the grid. Let's compare notes."

Sabin knew that speed was of the essence. The true investigative team wouldn't be here for a while, so the *Geneva* and the *Pueblo* needed to act. But they had to act together, and as accurately as they could.

Sabin had the five former members of foldspace investigation and rescue evaluate the information. She did the same.

And she discovered that Foucheux was right: there was something at the edge of the *Pueblo*'s last grid search that looked like one of the Fleet's ships. Oddly, it didn't have an active signature, but that could mean many things.

It could mean that the *Ivoire* was dead, with no power at all.

It could also mean that what they were looking at was a ship, but not one of the Fleet's.

"Is the computer finding anything else on its deep searches?" Sabin asked Wilmot. "Are we getting other strange readings?"

"No, sir," he said. "This is the only thing that could be a ship, according to the data we've analyzed so far."

No analysis could be complete in such a short period of time. There could be other things in the grid that they'd missed because of their focus on the *Ivoire*.

But all of that—if there were anything at all—would have to wait for the foldspace investigation and rescue team.

She needed to make a decision now.

"Tell the *Pueblo* we're going to focus our search on that part of the grid, and we're going to take a maximum of three minutes per search inside foldspace instead of one minute."

"Sir?" Wilmot asked. "The time—"

"I am aware of the time," Sabin said. "We don't have enough ships to double up, so we have to continue doing this as best we can."

Her heart was pounding. Three minutes in foldspace would seem like forever to the ship outside of foldspace. But it would also give her time—and Foucheux time—to figure out what, if anything, that reading on the sensors was.

"Take us into the last place the *Pueblo* was," Sabin said to Alvarez. "Then prepare to move quickly toward that blip.

If we read it as anything but one of our ships, we move back into position, and return to real space. Got that?"

She wanted everyone clear on the mission before they went in.

"Let the *Pueblo* know we're heading in," she said, and gave the order.

17

When they were inside foldspace, the blip on the *Pueblo*'s search grid did not seem like a blip at all. It looked solid.

Sabin's bridge crew worked quietly and quickly, shouting out information only when necessary.

The ship wasn't that far away from their position, and as they approached, it became clear they *were* looking at a ship.

One of the Fleet's ships.

But not the *Ivoire*. The *Ivoire*'s design was sleeker, with some of the design tweaks that Sabin herself had helped engineer.

Her heart continued to pound as they approached the ship.

It had no power; that was evident. And its *anacapa* wasn't working at all. No matter what system the *Geneva* used to see if the ship had an energy signature, they could find nothing.

It took less than a minute to get close enough to get a full visual on the ship.

Its center was gone; only the outer edges remained, giving it a ship-like shape, but no real heart.

No wonder she saw no evidence of the *anacapa*. There was no *anacapa* at all. The bridge was gone, engineering was gone, the heart of the ship was gone.

And it looked, from a cursory glance, as if the entire ship had somehow been ripped open. At some point, probably when the ship arrived in foldspace, it had hit something, done the thing everyone feared, and landed on top of, in the middle of, something else—an asteroid, space debris, or another ship.

No one survived.

Even if they had survived in the outer edges of the ship, they would not be alive now. Without that center core of the ship, the crew would have had only a few weeks to live. And judging by the design—what she could see of the design—those few weeks had expired years ago.

"Captain." Wilmot's voice was tight. "Look."

He zoomed on a section of the damaged ship, showing that section only to her. The name of the ship registered on her screen:

The *Sikkerhet*.

Sabin had finally found her father.

18

Somehow, Sabin remained calm. That detached feeling she'd had earlier when the *anacapa* first activated had returned. She knew that she had to captain the *Geneva*, and she had to continue on her mission.

Only the mission had changed.

They did have a ship to recover as well as one to find.

But their time had run out. They also had to return to real space.

Sabin got the *Geneva* back. Then she contacted Foucheux. Sabin almost asked for a private conference, but knew that was for her. It wasn't necessary and it would take too much time.

Foucheux appeared on one screen to the left of Sabin. Foucheux was tall and thin, and seemed more so on a two-dimensional screen. Her mocha-colored skin looked a bit gray, but that might be the lighting or the imagery.

Or she might be tired from the interruption of the respite period, just like everyone else had been.

She stood with her hands clasped behind her back. That posture, and the way that she had pulled back her black hair, made her seem more severe than usual.

"It's not the *Ivoire*," Sabin said, even though she suspected Foucheux had already seen the data. "It's the *Sikkerhet,* and it was destroyed long ago. I have no idea how it got to this part of foldspace or what that even means. The *Sikkerhet* has been missing for decades, and it was nowhere near this section of real space when it disappeared."

Her voice remained calm, normal, in control. She felt like three people—the captain of the *Geneva*, a little girl who had just realized her father was really and truly dead, and the woman who watched them both.

"Regulations require us to continue the search for the *Ivoire* and let recovery teams handle the *Sikkerhet*," Sabin said. Wilmot was watching her. She had a feeling that Charlie expected her to countermand regulations. "And in this instance, regulations absolutely apply. The *Sikkerhet* is beyond help, and any crew that survived either took lifepods elsewhere long ago, or expired when the ship got destroyed."

Her voice still remained calm. She felt calm. Or at least the captain part of her did, as did the observer part. The little girl had a metaphorical fist against her mouth to prevent an outburst, and wanted nothing more than to flee to her cabin right now.

There was no right now, not for grieving. Technically, Sabin should have done that a long, long time ago.

"So," Sabin said, "let's maintain our initial plan for the grid search and our initial timeline. I'll send the location of the *Sikkerhet* to the foldspace investigation and rescue team."

Foucheux nodded. Her posture didn't change, but her expression had softened. "I was going to suggest the same thing. But, let me be the first to say to you that I'm sorry."

Sabin had nearly interrupted. She didn't want her crew to know the meaning of the *Sikkerhet*. Nor did she want any more sympathy.

"Thank you," she said, and this time she had just a bit of wobble in her voice. "Now, let's get back to the search."

"We're on it," Foucheux said and signed off.

After a moment, the *Pueblo* disappeared into foldspace.

Sabin took a deep breath and sat down.

"Captain, did I miss something?" Ebedat asked. "Did something—"

"Nothing's amiss," Sabin said, trying to forestall the questions. "We continue the search. Please make sure that both Captain Cho, the *Alta*, and foldspace rescue know about the *Sikkerhet*."

"Yes, sir," Ebedat said. "Already done, sir."

"Good," Sabin said, and forced herself to focus, as she waited for the *Pueblo* to return.

19

"If I could discourage you from this path, I would," Major Zeller said, on the day he became her advisor.

They were sitting in his office on the *Brazza*, a blue-and-white planet visible through the gigantic window on the left side of the room. The *Brazza* was in orbit, while the Fleet tried to decide if the planet would become the next sector base location. A series of post-doctoral students were taking part in the studies, so someone in command believed it easier to have the *Brazza* in orbit than in its usual place near the bulk of the Fleet.

"You should go back to engineering, designing, and numbers," Zeller said. "You have a gift for them, and we need someone like you there."

Sabin hadn't expected his negativity, particularly since he was to be her advisor for the next few years.

"I tested well," she said. "In fact, I tested higher than anyone else this year."

"You did," he said. "Tests aren't everything."

"I know that," she said. "But I come from a long line of commanders. My father was a captain. My grandfather made general. My great-grandmother—"

"I'm aware of your family's history," Zeller said. "That's why we're talking. It's your family's history that makes me think you're not captain material."

She felt the shock all the way through her. No one had spoken to her like this before. Until this moment, everyone she had encountered, all of the administrators, instructors, and so many others believed she belonged in command.

"Excuse me?" she said, because she didn't know how else to respond.

"Ever since your father disappeared, you've been on a single-minded mission to find him," Zeller said. "Along the way, you have helped the Fleet. Your design for searches in foldspace is genius. The tweaks you've made to the *anacapa* systems and use are valuable. The designs you've added to the ships are both luxurious and comfortable. But none of that will make you a good leader. In fact, I think you'll be a terrible one."

Her face warmed. If she got angry now, though—or, at least, let him see how angry she already was—she would prove him right.

"My father has been gone a long time," she said.

"Yes, he has," Zeller said. "But I know how this goes. I've lost people too. I was on the first team sent—using your methods—to try to find the *Sikkerhet*. I volunteered because I had family on that ship."

His expression changed just a little, saddened, then hardened again. This was not a man with whom she could speak of shared sympathy.

"The hardest part of being a leader, Victoria," Zeller said, using her real first name, which no one ever did, and it made her feel even smaller, "is not decisions, but the attrition. You will lose people. They will fall away like parts off a damaged ship. They will get angry and move planetside, they will transfer, or they will die in battle."

She knew that. She had already lived through it. Even children lost friends when ships went down. The losses had been part of her life, like they were part of everyone's life here in the Fleet.

"But some of them, Victoria, will disappear. Literally disappear. You won't know what happened to them ever. They will be like ghosts who haunt you through your entire career."

"I know that," she said.

He gave her a contemptuous smile. "No, you don't. You think you do because we all lose people, we lose things, we lose ships. But you don't, because you've never been responsible for the loss. You've never ordered a ship to go into a dangerous maneuver or into foldspace or into a battle where no one emerges alive. The responsibility is what's different, Victoria. And the responsibility makes you second-guess everything."

She willed herself not to move. She suspected this conversation was more about him than it was about her. He was probably moved off the career track into academic administration because he couldn't handle the results of his own orders.

"When you start second-guessing," he said, "everything you do, everything you are, is about that ghost. Every captain has one. Generals have dozens. But they acquire them during their commands. They lose people. And not every leader mentally survives those losses."

She was convinced now: this was about him, not her. But she listened.

She had no other choice.

"You already have a ghost," he said. "One that you can't let go of. Your entire life has been about finding your father, and he can't be found. He is *gone*, Victoria, and nothing you do, no search patterns you develop, no tweaks you make to the *anacapa* drive, no command you give when your ship needs to go to foldspace, will ever change that."

She wasn't sure if she should respond. But he had paused for several seconds now, so she said, "I know that, sir."

"Intellectually, yes, you know that. Emotionally, you do not. And someday, you will risk your entire crew because of your father. You will make a decision that has nothing to do with now, and everything to do with that loss. It might not seem obvious. It might seem totally unrelated. But it won't be. And more people will die."

She wanted to say sarcastically, *Thank you for your belief in me, sir*, but she didn't.

Instead, she silently vowed she would prove him wrong.

"I'm not leaving the officer training program," she said. "If I wash out, fine. But I want to do this. I think I'll be good at it. I think I'll be better at it than anything else I've ever done."

He shook his head slightly, as if he couldn't believe her arrogance. Well, she couldn't believe his. Who was he to tell her who she was and who she would be?

"I'm going to be watching you," he said. "The moment I see that ghost making decisions for you, I'm pulling you out. Is that clear?"

She wondered how he would know. Would he fudge results? Would he see a "ghost" where there was none?

But she knew better than to ask. She remained as still as she possibly could, so he wouldn't see her steeling herself for battle with him.

"Yes, sir," she said calmly. "That's clear."

Technically, she should have thanked him. Technically, she should have told him that he was doing the entire Fleet a favor by keeping an eye on her.

But that was admitting weakness.

She wasn't going to admit weakness. Especially not now.

She wanted to command—and she would.

And she would be so much better than Zeller ever was, than Zeller ever could be.

But she didn't tell him that either.

Instead, she would show him. Every single day, for the rest of her life.

20

THE *GENEVA* AND THE *PUEBLO* CONTINUED THE GRID search, but Sabin knew after the fiftieth iteration they would find nothing. No trace of the *Ivoire*.

She tried not to feel dispirited, and when the emotion threatened to overwhelm her, she privately blamed it all on the confirmation of her father's death.

She didn't let any emotion show. She did her job, coldly and efficiently, knowing she could tend to her emotions later.

Even after the foldspace investigation and rescue team arrived, even after they failed to find the *Ivoire* with a thorough by-the-books search, she held her emotions back.

They did her no good. They certainly didn't help her, or anyone, find Coop.

The *Geneva* took part in a lot of the background investigation, providing support, ferrying teams to various parts of the Ukhandan sector.

And all the while, the foldspace investigation and rescue team searched, doing the math over and over again, trying to find a hole in the logic, replaying the telemetry sent by the *Ivoire*, the coordinates, the estimates—and finding nothing.

Just like the ships that searched for the *Sikkerhet* found nothing all those years ago.

When it became clear that the *Geneva's* role would be downsized, Sabin took some time off—actual time off.

She got some sleep. And she spoke to a mandatory grief counselor. She was proud of herself; she didn't lie. She said the discovery of her father's ship brought everything back up, and created as many questions as it answered.

The remaining information systems on the *Sikkerhet* were corrupted, the life pods were in place in the intact portions of the ship, but all of that meant nothing considering how much time had passed.

The foldspace investigation and rescue team brought the *Sikkerhet* back to real space, and would take it to Sector Base V for study. There they would figure out what the information systems said, what happened in the last few hours of the ship, and how it got to that part of foldspace.

For all anyone knew, that part of foldspace was the part ships went to when they activated the *anacapa* decades ago. Or maybe it was easily accessed from the part of real space where the *Sikkerhet* had been when it disappeared.

No one knew, but they did know they had to answer some questions. Sabin knew that she needed the questions answered as well.

Because, she figured, if they found out what happened to the *Sikkerhet*, they might end up with more information in their search for the *Ivoire*.

That search would continue for months, maybe years. Already a mathematics and theoretical physics team had come in to watch the imagery of the *Ivoire* in the moments before it vanished. They were timing the last message, and figuring out why it had reached the ships before the *Ivoire* vanished, since those two things should have happened simultaneously.

The hope was that they would figure out the differential, use it in the equations that sent ships into a particular part of foldspace, and find the *Ivoire*.

The *Alta* had sent another diplomatic ship to work with the Xenth in locating the ships that had attacked the *Ivoire*. If a team from the Fleet got to investigate those ships' weapons systems, they might figure out how the weapons interacted with the *Ivoire's anacapa*, *if* those weapons did indeed interact with the *anacapa*, and maybe come up with some answers that way.

The *Geneva* was to help transport the *Sikkerhet* to Sector Base V. Sabin knew that she had received a charity mission, one that would let her find some answers slowly, and for once in her life, she didn't care.

Because she had finally come to some conclusions.

As the *Geneva* traveled back to Sector Base V, she asked for a private conference with General Zeller.

She spoke to him from her private communications room in her captain's suite, the same room in which she had spoken to Coop night after night after night.

She didn't miss the sexual side of her relationship with Coop—that had happened only a few times per year—but she missed the friendship, the ability to consult with some-one who had a similar job but a different point of view.

She felt all alone now, in a way she had never felt alone before.

But she didn't tell Zeller that.

Instead, when his disapproving face appeared on her screen, she actually smiled at him.

"I'm finally going to do what you want, General," she said, after the initial niceties ended.

His gaze kept moving away from her image, as if something else in the room interested him more than any conversation with her could. "And that would be?"

"I'm resigning my commission. I'm stepping down as captain of the *Geneva*."

His entire posture changed. His gaze snapped forward, meeting hers.

"That is not what I want," he said. "You have become one of the best captains in the Fleet. You proved me wrong long ago, Captain Sabin, and even on this most difficult mission, you kept your focus on the task at hand, setting your personal problems aside and rising to a standard that few captains achieved."

She had waited years for praise like that from him. Her cheeks warmed as her face flushed. But the praise was no longer relevant.

"Thank you, General," she said, "but I realized on this last trip that you were right: My father's disappearance has haunted me. It still does. We don't entirely understand what happened—"

"We're pretty sure that the ship collided with something in foldspace as it arrived," Zeller said. "Every captain's nightmare."

"Yes," Sabin said. "It is, and they're probably right. But I want to know."

"You can get reports. Your talents would be wasted working on the remains of the *Sikkerhet*. Let the technicians do it—"

"General," she said gently. "I've acquired a new ghost on this trip."

To his credit, he stopped speaking and frowned. "Someone on the *Ivoire*?" he asked, keeping the question both professional and delicate.

"Captain Cooper and I were good friends," she said, unwilling to explain more. "I believe if I return to foldspace and *anacapa* research, I might be able to find him."

"We've lost one excellent captain on this trip," Zeller said. "We can't lose you as well."

A month ago, these comments would have angered her. She would have wanted to know why he hadn't said such things to her before, why he had kept his evaluations to himself.

Or she would have demanded to know why he believed her good now, instead of earlier. She could almost hear her own voice, strained, angry: *Am I a better captain now that you're short a captain, General? Or are you supposed to say this to keep me in line?*

But she didn't have the energy or the desire for that kind of confrontation.

"General," she said gently, "my full attention will never again be on the *Geneva* and that, by definition, will make me a bad captain. I'm going to resign my commission, and you can't talk me out of it. If you value my work, please help me secure a good spot on the teams investigating the *Sikkerhet* and the disappearance of the *Ivoire*."

His expression was flat. Only his eyes moved, as if he could see through the camera into her soul.

"I have never understood you," he said. "I always thought I did, but I don't."

"I disagree, General. You believed me obsessed with my father's disappearance, and I was. When I realized I could learn no more, I put myself in a position to emulate him. And now that we have information again, I want to return to research."

Zeller shook his head. "Your father wouldn't understand this."

"Probably not," she said. "I think it would make him angry."

She didn't add the rest. She had finally realized that she was her mother's daughter as well as her father's. Unlike her mother, Sabin thrived in a military environment. But unlike her father, she had to choose her own path, and if that path deviated from the norm, she had to follow the new path instead of trudging along the old.

Amazing that a double loss—learning her father was truly dead and suspecting that Coop was as well—would help her discover who she really was.

Perhaps that was what living was all about, using the good and the bad to determine the essence of one's self.

"I'll be more useful in research," she said. "Of course, I will remain on the *Geneva* until the Fleet can provide a suitable replacement."

"I don't think anyone has resigned a captain's commission after such a success, Sabin," Zeller said. "Not in all the years of the Fleet."

She didn't believe that was true. There were centuries of Fleet history, and so much had disappeared into legend.

"I don't consider what happened in foldspace a success, sir," she said. "We lost the *Ivoire*."

"And found a ship that we had thought gone forever, Captain," Zeller said. "We wouldn't have found it without you. The foldspace rescue team says they might have dismissed that blip on their equipment. They think you and Captain Foucheux saw things they did not, and they must change their algorithms accordingly."

This was one of the reasons that Sabin had to return to research and foldspace investigation. The method of doing things had become more important than the purpose for doing those things.

The teams no longer thought of the lives hanging in the balance. They thought about the probabilities for success.

And with that realization, she finally understood what Zeller was telling her.

There was only one person who could have found the *Sikkerhet* on this mission, one person whose thinking was both rigid enough to conduct a grid search and creative enough to explore all the possibilities.

That was why he considered her mission a success.

"I am going to see if we can invent a new position for you, Captain," Zeller said. "We need something better in investigations, and we need someone of command rank who can run that new system. Tell me you'll keep your captain's commission and accept the reassignment."

"Only if I may focus on research, sir," she said.

"Research, investigation, and the technology itself. I'll see if we can change the *Geneva's* designation so she can be the ship in charge of that part of our team."

"Sir, the *Geneva's* not equipped for the kind of work we would need to do," she said. "We would need a newer ship, one outfitted especially for us."

His eyes narrowed, that disapproving look she knew so well. He had once accused her of taking what little she was offered, and ungratefully asking for ten times as much.

She had just done so now.

But she didn't take back her request.

"My instinct is to say no, Captain," he said. "But I have learned that my instinct always discounts you. So I will see what I can do."

"Thank you, sir," she said as he signed off.

She sat in her small backup control room for several minutes afterward, staring at the blank screen.

For the first time in their careers, neither Zeller nor Sabin had won the argument with each other. They had compromised in a way neither of them would have thought possible two decades before.

She was starting something new, remaking something old into a brand new part of the Fleet.

And, sadly, the first thing she wanted to do was tell Coop. He might not understand her choice, but he would give her an intelligent and lively discussion. He would let her know what she hadn't thought of, and what she needed to do to make the experiment work.

She closed her eyes for just a moment.

She would remain a captain, and the loneliness would still be a large part of her life.

Maybe even larger now, without Coop.

As a young girl, she had needed her father back. She couldn't imagine life without him.

As an adult woman, she wanted Coop back. But she could easily imagine life without him. It wasn't just something she would have chosen.

None of this was.

And here was the difference between her childhood and now: If her research found Coop alive, she still would retain a job in research and foldspace investigation. If they had found her father before she quit school, she would have become someone else.

Funny how the events of one's life changed that life.

Coop understood that. He seemed to fathom how wisdom was hard-earned, not something someone else could impart and believe that another person would get.

Maybe that was why the Fleet's insistence on stepping into life in other cultures bothered him so much. Because he hadn't even been certain he understood his own life.

She wished she could tell him that she finally realized what he had been telling her all those months ago.

And, in acknowledging the feeling she had, she realized also that she believed, deep down, she would never get the chance to tell him. Even if her research led to his ship's discovery forty years from now, she suspected Coop would not be on it, just like her father hadn't been on his ship.

Hard-won understanding.

It wasn't quite the death of hope—part of her still hoped that Coop was alive somewhere.

It was more like the application of hope.

She wanted to make sure that no one else—child, adult, crew member, captain—would ever lose a loved one to foldspace again.

It was probably a vain hope.

But it would keep her going, for at least another forty years.

Read more in Kristine Kathryn Rusch's award-winning
Diving Universe and find out the fate of the *Ivoire*
in *City of Ruins*, on sale now.

Be the first to know!

Just sign up for the Kristine Kathryn Rusch newsletter,
and keep up with the latest news, releases
and so much more—even the occasional giveaway.

So, what are you waiting for?
To sign up go to kristinekathrynrusch.com.

But wait! There's more. Sign up for the WMG
Publishing newsletter, too, and get the latest news
and releases from all of the WMG authors and lines,
including Kristine Grayson, Kris Nelscott, Dean
Wesley Smith, *Fiction River: An Original Anthology
Magazine, Pulphouse Fiction Magazine, Smith's
Monthly,* and so much more.

To sign up, go to wmgpublishing.com.

ABOUT THE AUTHOR

New York Times bestselling author Kristine Kathryn Rusch writes in almost every genre. Generally, she uses her real name (Rusch) for most of her writing. Under that name, she publishes bestselling science fiction and fantasy, award-winning mysteries, acclaimed mainstream fiction, controversial nonfiction, and the occasional romance. Her novels have made bestseller lists around the world and her short fiction has appeared in eighteen best of the year collections. She has won more than twenty-five awards for her fiction, including the Hugo, *Le Prix Imaginales*, the *Asimov's* Readers Choice award, and the *Ellery Queen Mystery Magazine* Readers Choice Award.

To keep up with everything she does, go to kriswrites.com and sign up for her newsletter. To track her many pen names and series, see their individual websites (krisnelscott.com, kristinegrayson.com, retrievalartist.com, divingintothewreck.com, fictionriver.com, pulphousemagazine.com).

The Retrieval Artist Universe

(Reading Order)